# ACTING THE PART

## LOVE UNDER LOCKDOWN SERIES BOOK 7

## ANDREA HURTT

# CHAPTER 1

L isa set down her suitcase and looked around the living room of her temporary apartment. Her agent had assured her it was a wonderful location in a safe neighborhood in Vancouver, with a view of the harbor to die for. What she didn't tell her was the next-door neighbor had no manners. It was almost 11 pm PST, three hours past her normal body clock time, and next door was blaring music like they were having a party.

She sighed with distaste.

Walking around, she took in the tiny apartment. Immediately to the left of the entrance was a bathroom, a few more steps in and the galley kitchen was to her right. The living room filled the rest of the space. Just past the bathroom on the left was the one and only bedroom.

*At least it has a king-sized bed.*

She went to the glass door in the bedroom and slid it open. Chilled March air rushed over her, the scent of brine mixed in. The next-door neighbor's music blocked any sound of the busy road below.

*Seriously?*

She wanted to go bust on their door; she was exhausted and

just needed to sleep. It didn't sound like that was going to happen. Lisa returned to the room, closing the door behind her. It helped slightly with the noise, but not enough to appease her. Grabbing her suitcase from the entryway, she noticed a note on the kitchen bar.

*Lisa, I hope you are well and this role brings you a little joy. If not, I left a large bottle of sweet red wine in the fridge for you. Best of luck, Debbie.*

HER AGENT always looked out for her, leaving her bottles of wine, a box of fancy chocolates, or finding a place with a hot tub. Debbie picked the best roles for her. Lisa had yet come into one she didn't like.

*Until now.*

That wasn't true. It wasn't the role that worried her. It was the lead actor in the show.

He'd gotten a reputation for being a player. He could have any woman he wanted.

And he wanted them all.

Whether or not it was true, Lisa didn't care. She would not be a notch on his bedpost. She was there to do a job. Play a part and move on.

She normally took acting gigs in Atlanta and the outlying area, close to home. But Vancouver was becoming known as North Hollywood, and she needed to make her name known there. Her role on *Demons Within Us* was a one-time deal, but she would be in almost every scene.

That was huge for her.

This would open doors for her that no other role could ever do.

But one scene she dreaded. It wouldn't be her first, or last time acting such an intimate scene, but to do it with *him*, that was another story.

Kyle Gibson was ruggedly handsome. He kept his sandy brown hair cut close except on top. There, he had enough to run your hands through, enough to grab a hold on and give a tug. His eyes were deep green, like the forest at twilight. His body was made for all the things she didn't want to think about. And she was going to have to press her mostly naked body against his.

*Guess that's the best thing about not liking him. I won't be getting a female boner.*

An hour later she was curled up in bed, ready for Mr. Sandman to come to visit. The hot shower had helped relax her sore muscles, but now she was overheated. Lisa crawled out of bed and slipped to the sliding glass door.

*Maybe some cold fresh air will help.*

It surprised her the noise from next door had lowered drastically. It wasn't gone, just less. She stepped out onto her balcony, the breeze from the bay cooling her body, but making her more awake. Her place was high enough from the ground that if anyone below looked up, they wouldn't be able to see she only had on a thin nightshirt. She left her newfound haven to travel to the kitchen and poured herself a glass of the lovely wine her agent had left for her. It might be the only thing that helped her sleep.

She returned to her balcony, and a moan escaped her lips when the sweet red liquid entered her mouth.

\* \* \*

To say it had been a long day would be an understatement. If it could go wrong, it did. Everything from the neighbors bitching about the daytime noise, when they'd had plenty of notification there would be filming, to the food truck not showing up.

*Bad gas, my ass.*

To top it all off, they didn't have enough extra's show up for a crowd scene.

*Thank God our episode's leading lady gets here tomorrow.*

Lisa Kay was only working this one episode, and she was in every scene but the one he'd filmed that day. She would make the hard days, well, hard. But in a much more pleasant way.

Kyle had been following her career for months. He'd seen her, once, at a film festival in Park City, UT, and needed to get close to her. But never got the chance. He'd watch her from afar, appreciating not only her beauty, damn, that ass, but the way she worked the crowd.

*Can she work me, too?*

He'd begged to have her as a guest on the show. And they'd agreed. He would even get a sex scene with her. He couldn't have asked for more.

Except for the day to have been better.

Once he'd gotten back to his apartment, he turned on his music, the playlist the neighbors hated but helped calm his nerves. He couldn't explain why it helped. It didn't matter.

Around one am, he finally felt back to himself and turned the sound down. Not off. Just down. And stepped out onto his balcony for some much needed fresh air. He breathed in deep, letting the salt in the air coat his lungs. Growing up in the mid-south, he didn't get much sea air before getting the role of Gene Priest.

He took in another breath, stretching his arms skyward, arching his back, letting his body further relax. Rolling his head from side to side, he realized he wasn't alone. On the balcony next to his was a beautiful Nymph.

Her body was facing forward, but she was looking to the right, away from him.

Her black hair ruffled around, dancing in the wind. Dressed in only a nightshirt, it was barely there. Although it covered her from neck to thigh, it was practically sheer. He could see she was chilled. Her nipples peeking through the thin fabric. He felt his cock jerk in excitement.

*Woh, dude. Calm the shit down.*

She turned her head in his direction and he almost fell over.

*Lisa Kay!*

His heart thundered, and he fought to get his bearings. Doing the only thing his mind could wrap around, he gave her his best smile.

"Fuck you," was her reply, followed by a hasty retreat inside.

*What?*

He didn't understand. Most women blushed profusely when he smiled. That was usually all it took to get them where he wanted them. But not Lisa.

*Why?*

Now he was more determined than ever to have her.

MORNING COULDN'T COME SOON ENOUGH for Kyle. He'd have Lisa on set and mostly naked before the day was over.

Dick, their director, was very courteous with the female guest when a sex scene was called for. It would be a closed set, the bare minimal production team, and it was always the first thing they filmed.

Kyle understood why. Because the women always seemed to get a boner for him, and by the time the week of shooting was over, they really were trying to get into his pants. It made the sex scenes a little too real. So Dick switched gears after the third season. Now the sex scenes were done first. And he was all for it.

Stepping out of the shower, he heard her water start. Kyle couldn't help but recall the taut nipples peeking from her nightshirt.

*Are they pink or more cherry colored?*

*I bet they are soft as a rose petal.*

*I just want to taste.*

His cock hardened as he thought about standing in the shower with her. Their bodies slick with water and soap, sliding across each other, bringing them both to a frenzy.

*Chill.*

He rushed to his bedroom to get ready for the day, needing to get away from the lustful thoughts she was filling his head with.

An hour later, Kyle was standing outside the building, waiting for the studio car to pick him up when she stepped up to him.

"Good morning." He smiled at her. "I'm Kyle," he introduced himself.

As if she didn't know. Everyone knew Kyle Gibson. He was the hottest man on tv. If you didn't know him, you lived in a cave.

"I know," she mumbled.

"We're staying in the same building. Obviously. But I thought you should know I'm right next door, in case you need anything."

"I know you are. Can you please keep the music to a normal level today? I'd like to hear myself think tonight."

He laughed. "So that's why you told me to fuck off last night!"

"No. I'd had a long day and your music didn't help." She looked down at her phone then back up at him, her cerulean blue eyes piercing him. "I take it we are riding together."

*I'd like to ride with her.*

*Seriously, dude. Calm down.*

"Looks like it." He held the car door open for her when the black Escalade pulled up to the curb.

She slid onto the seat, and he rushed to enter the other side. He couldn't help but notice her crossing and uncrossing her legs.

*Is her body reacting like mine is?*

*I swear I can smell the excitement on her.*

His eyes slipped up her long, lean legs; drawn there by the

way she kept tugging at her skirt. It was not made for a woman with legs like hers.

*I want those legs around me.*

They sat in silence, neither one willing to break the tension until the driver pulled up to the building that held the sound stage.

"I guess I'll be seeing you soon, in the back of my car," Kyle leaned in to whisper in her ear. He could see the gooseflesh erupt over her skin. He smiled before climbing out of the Escalade and off to his personal trailer.

# CHAPTER 2

"**A**re you fucking kidding me? This cocky bastard is putting the moves on me before we have to film a sex scene? In the back of his character's car!"

She was bitching to the makeup artist who had earbuds in, the music so loud she knew the woman hadn't heard a word she said. But it made her feel better.

"Everything I have ever heard about Kyle Gibson has been about his need to bed every woman that comes on the set! I won't be one of them."

The girl pulled her earbud out. "I'm sorry, were you talking to me?"

"No, just bitching about Kyle."

"Oh, he's just the sweetest thing! Probably one of the most humble actors I have ever worked with, and I have been doing this a while. He'll treat you right, don't you worry."

*Don't worry?*

*Are we talking about the same guy?*

*Mr. Playboy?*

She shook her head, trying to clear out the irritating thoughts.

She was about to become Missy Grey, the one episode love interest of Gene Priest.

Missy's backstory had her living in a convent from a young age because of her 'visions'. She's called to Sioux Falls, where Gene is on a case, to help figure out what happened to a small-town girl, using her abilities. She finds out her visions are actually psychic readings. While there, Gene seduces Missy, and she loses her virginity to him in the back of his car.

That's what they were filming that day.

The makeup artist was giving her a fresh, virginal look, or so she said when she had begun. Lisa looked at herself in the mirror and was shocked.

She did look innocent!

Her eyes were bright, and her cheeks flushed.

Lisa brought her shoulders forward slightly, giving the look a bit more. Being innocent was as much in the makeup as the body language.

"Perfect! Let's get you over to wardrobe!"


AN HOUR later she stepped onto the closed set. Looking around, you'd never know they were indoors. The 1965 black Ford Mustang with gold/orange stripes sat in what looked like an empty cornfield, drying out stalks filling in the background. Part of the top of the car was cut out to allow the camera to film the interior scenes. The lighting made the warehouse feel like it was twilight in Iowa. It was beautiful.

"Ms. Kay," the director, Dick called out to her. "We'll do a few run-throughs first. I know you are a seasoned actor, but I still like to go over things for people."

She listened as he told her everything she already knew. But she was attentive, in case there was an unexpected twist in his direction. She'd been so focused on Dick's voice, she didn't hear Kyle step up behind her.

"Good morning, Lisa," he whispered.

Gooseflesh erupted along her skin, whether from the heat of his breath, or the sensual tone in his voice, she didn't know. Or care. She stepped out of his reach and closer to Dick.

"Let's get you two set up in the car. The scene breaks right into the heat of the moment, so that's gonna be a nice transition."

*Nice for who?*

Sex scenes were never fun to film. The full-time cast had it the hardest, though. The team they knew all too well, would look around awkwardly, hating to see people they know naked. You'd count beats in your head; kiss, count to four, turn head, count to four, kiss, and so on.

It was as far from sexy as it got.

"Let's do this," Kyle said, opening the door and letting her climb in first.

The moment they were settled, Lisa propped up by her arms, her knees bent, and her bare feet up on the glass, she knew things would be different. She understood the necessity of the skirt for easy access, but would an innocent really wear a skirt like what they put her in? It barely covered her cookie when she got in the car.

Then Kyle settled between her legs. The rough texture of his jeans rubbed against the sensitive skin of her inner thigh, sending unwanted vibrations through her body.

She'd done her fair share of sex scenes. And this one already showed her it would be like nothing she'd ever done before.

He pulled her in for a kiss. His tongue danced with hers, even in the strict production style. When they kissed, their lips weren't fully meeting, he kissed only her upper lip. It was the way kissing had always been done in film.

And yet, he ignited a passion in her.

*No! Cool down, chicka!*

He pulled her closer and laid her back on the seat, readjusting himself on top of her. His kisses trailed from her mouth to her ear.

Lisa moaned in pleasure as his tongue swirled around inside her ear. He sucked on her lobe before moving to her neck.

Her back arched up into him.

Kyle's hand slid the strap of her bra and tank top off her shoulder and kissed the exposed skin while his other hand cupped her breast. His thumb rubbed back and forth across her sensitive nipples. She was afraid she'd poke his eye out with them.

Lisa found her way under his shirt and pulled it up over his head.

His chest was smooth and bare. And rock hard.

He leaned down, kissing her again as he ground against her.

She reached between them and slowly unbuckled his belt.

Kyle pushed her skirt up and ran his hand over the silk panties she wore.

She moaned at the feel of his fingers caressing her.

*Why do I like him touching me like this?*

*Oh God, don't stop.*

"Cut!" Dick called out. The director stepped up to the car and opened the door. "Damn, you two. That was a little too hot. Can we try that again and keep it PG-13."

KYLE HAD to step away for a moment. How many sex scenes had he done on this show in the past few years? He couldn't say. He'd lost count. It seemed like there was one every episode yet, this was the first time he'd needed to walk away.

*What is it about this woman?*

He had earned an unwanted reputation over the years, that he was a player. What most people didn't know, he was the one being played. Every love interest they'd had on the show for his character, wanted to bed him before their time was over. He made that mistake once, sleeping with an actress. And he swore never to do it again.

But Lisa was getting under his skin.

He wanted her.

No. He needed her.

He dared a glance over at her, watching her sip water through a straw. His balls tightened and his cock jerked awake.

How was he going to survive the week?

"Kyle! Let's go. Reset!"

He took a deep breath and returned to the car.

"Gene," the director called to him using his character's name. "Remember, she is a virgin you are seducing. Make it slow, deliberate. You want to drive her to the brink of extinction. You want her to want you so bad she's willing to break her covenant and give you her flower."

Kyle looked down at Lisa, back flat on the seat, her black hair lying around her like a silk sheet, her eyes hooded.

*She's the one seducing me.*

He wasn't sure why he had that thought. Lisa was not seducing him, not like all the others had. She was downright cold to him.

Missy was seducing Gene.

"Quiet on the set."

They ran the scene three times before Dick let them break. Kyle had every plan to run straight to his trailer and take a cold shower but was stopped by the director.

"Hey, Kyle. I know you know what you're doing, but this ain't no porno. You two gotta cool it down. We haven't needed to bust out the hardware to steam the windows of the car. You two are doing it all on your own."

"I'm sorry. I… I don't know what to say."

"It's okay, half the crew is walking around with boners. Lisa

Kay is hot. And cold. That's what is driving us all nuts. It looks like she is getting to you too. Good luck. Be back on set in 15."

The next three hours were hell.

Dick was right.

She was cold.

Kyle had to take a mental step back and look at it from an actor's point of view.

*Hell, I am an actor, why am I fucking this up?*

You had to be cold when doing a scene like this. Otherwise, it was… well… Soft porn.

*Isn't that more or less what Dick was saying?*

*Cool it down.*

She cooled things all the way down. After their last break, she came back as a different woman. She was ready to get the scene over and move on. Only one more take and it was in the can.

Back in the shared car, she said nothing as they rode back.

Instead of heading to the elevator, he wasn't sure he could handle being alone in another tight space with her for a while, he took off for a long walk.

The chill in the March night air helped cool his overheated body. Kyle had been an actor for most of his life. He had played some epic roles, including a sex slave on a soap opera, when he was barely legal. This shouldn't be bothering him so much.

Close to midnight, he finally made his way back to the tall building he called home and entered his apartment.

Sleep seemed to elude him. He tossed and turned all night, finally drifting off to sleep as the sun was beginning to rise.

# CHAPTER 3

Morning light slipped through the slit in the curtains, waking Kyle up with a jolt. He glanced at the clock. 9 am.

*Shit!*

In all the excitement of the day before, he's forgotten to set his alarm. They scheduled him for a set time of 10 am. Picking up his phone, he sent a quick text to the assistant director.

KYLE: Sorry, I overslept. I might be a little late.

CHUCK: Dude, didn't you check your voicemail? No filming. They shut us down.

KYLE: What are you talking about?

CHUCK: Don't you watch the news?

*Seriously? Over this virus that's hitting the world? But Vancouver hasn't seen a single case yet.*

KYLE: I thought we were gonna work through this. We're still good, right?

CHUCK: Not anymore. They shut the border down. No coming or going. Since we've got production people in Bellingham, they can't get here, we can't film.

KYLE: How long?

CHUCK: Indefinitely.

KYLE: Should I get a flight home? Back to the U.S.?

CHUCK: Bud, you're stuck. Might wanna check the news.

Kyle sat in his bed, staring at the wall. Lockdown. He couldn't go anywhere. He climbed out of bed and headed to the kitchen. Pulling open the fridge, he glanced at the contents. Other than only having a few bottles of wine left, he was rather well-stocked.

*What the fuck am I supposed to do with myself?*

*Lisa Kay is right next door.*

*Go woo her!*

He knew that wasn't the wisest idea. He avoided any off-stage interaction if possible. He slipped into his favorite workout gear and headed to the gym in the building. He needed to feel something other than the intense sexual tension the woman in the apartment next to him was causing. Even if it was just severe muscle strain.

* * *

"I'm sorry, Lisa, but you're gonna be in Vancouver for a while."

Her agent sounded upset, but it thrilled her. Were they extending her time on *Demons Within Us*? It happened to another actor that was only suppose to be on two episodes, but became a series regular.

"That's great! Am I staying on DWU, or…" She didn't get to finish her thought out loud.

"Babe. You haven't watched the news at all, have you?"

Lisa scoffed. Why would she watch the news in a town she would only be in for a week?

"No, why?"

Debbie chuckled from the other side of the line. "We're officially in lockdown. No coming or going. You're only allowed to leave your home for essentials, like food."

"Shit, how long?" She felt her heart thunder in her chest.

"Who knows? Weeks, Months. It just depends."

"Months? I only have a bottle of wine! Filming ran late yesterday, thank you to Kyle and his fucking cock! Can't you get me on a flight home? I'm assuming there is no filming them."

"No. On both accounts. They ground flights for everything but essential travel. You're stuck. I've got your apartment secured for as long as you're there. But you need to go get groceries. And wear a mask. Look online for ideas. I gotta go. Good luck, babe!"

Her agent ended the call, leaving her hanging.

*What the fuck am I supposed to do?*


"PAPER TOWELS. Don't have any. Scarves. Nope." She was scanning the internet on her laptop, looking for ways to cover her face. "Bandana. Yeah, right? Bra cup. Really? My bra?" She only had one with her. She didn't need more than that. Wardrobe supplied anything she needed on camera, she brought just the essentials to get her to and from the set.

But she considered High-Risk because of her asthma, so she knew she needed to come up with something.

*My bra it is.*

In the kitchen, she found a pair of scissors and followed the directions on Pinterest and cut up her favorite red bra. She found a safety pin in the bottom of her purse and used that where she couldn't sew it.

Lisa noticed Vancouver was a ghost town, as she walked the five blocks to Whole Foods. Robson Street was usually bustling with people, coming and going between the many restaurants and top-end shopping stores. Everything was closed.

Except for Whole Foods and Safeway.

Lisa got the essentials, hoping it would last at least two weeks.

. . .

WALKING BACK, she struggled not to drop the eight bags she carried. She was trying to push the button to call the elevator when *he* stepped up to her.

"Looks like you could use a little help." His voice was kind, yet eluded raw sexuality. "Let me get that for you." He reached in front of her to press the button.

*Oh, my!*

*Arm candy.*

*No! Don't look at him like that!*

*Didn't you learn anything yesterday?*

Her eyes followed from his brawny hands, up to his lickable bicep, taking in the intricate bird tattoo, to his shoulder, and finally his face. He showed no signs of distress after their encounter the day before.

Filming had gotten the better of her. She had never had her hormones so up in arms as she did that day. When they took a short break after the first run-through, she'd had to find a bathroom and... well... release some pressure.

Never in her life had she felt so unprofessional.

"Can you press the button please?" she muffled through the fabric of her bra.

*Oh shit! He's seeing my bra. On my face. I feel so stupid.*

They stepped into the elevator, he continued on, his voice like melted butter. "That's a lot of food. Are you having company over? A dinner party, perhaps?"

"Quarantine, dumbass." She couldn't help but reply. "Why aren't we moving? I can't get stuck in this fucking elevator with you!"

He reached out and pressed their floor number.

"Seriously? We've just been standing here? Didn't you think to press our floor? Are you that big of an idiot?" As soon as the words escaped her mouth, she wished she could shove them back in. This guy was the lead on one of the most popular tv shows filmed in Vancouver, and she couldn't afford to piss him off. He could make one phone call and get her on the blacklist. She took a deep breath and let it out slowly. She had to get over what had happened earlier in the day. It was no one's fault but her own. Or her hormones, as she was glad to blame.

"I'm sorry. That was uncalled for. It's just… I have perishables that I really need to get in the fridge."

"Like I said, that's a lot of food," he teased. The doors opened to their floor. "I'd really love the company, if you wanna have dinner together. I'll bring dessert." They'd reached her door. "Let me take some of those off your hands." He didn't wait, he just grabbed all her bags, allowing her to open the door.

She slipped her key back into her front pocket and tried to take her groceries back.

"I've got it," was all he replied, heading into her place.

*Sneaky bastard.*

"Looks just like mine, but opposite. My kitchen is on the left, and yours is on the right. But," he dropped all her bags on the counter and continued on further. "Looks like our headboards are up against each other." He turned and smiled at her, dimples playing peek-a-boo in his cheeks.

She was sure hers flushed red with heat. It wasn't the only part of her body affected by that smile.

*Damn it, no! I won't succumb to his charms!*

"So, dinner? What time should I be over? Should I bring a bottle of wine?"

*But I don't wanna play nice.*

"Eight would be fine. And yes. Bring a bottle of wine. But nothing too dry."

"I can do that. And dessert. I've got that covered." He slipped closer to her door, stopping when his hand was on the nob. "I hope you like chocolate and whip cream." He winked at her and left, leaving her with her jaw on the floor.

*Chocolate and whipped cream? He's got it covered. Covered on what?*

. . .

LISA SAT in the large tub, a glass of wine sitting on the edge, mostly empty now, with the water starting to chill. When she'd gotten in, she told herself not to shave her legs. If she didn't shave, she wouldn't be tempted to do something stupid. She'd already shaved that morning, their filming was rather intimate, but what the hell.

"I already said, I won't be a notch in his bedpost," she growled at her empty glass, the very last drop of wine teasing her. The sound of her voice echoed off the white tiled wall. "So why am I working so hard to look nice?" She'd sugar scrubbed her entire body, shaved, washed her hair, and soaked until the water was cold. She'd taken great care to set her hair and apply her makeup.

Lisa had only brought what she needed to get her to the set, so it limited her clothing options for entertaining.

*I don't need to impress him!*

No, but she needed to make him happy.

He needed to like her.

Kyle could make or break her career in Vancouver.

*What the fuck am I making for dinner?*

She spent so much time stressing out about how she looked, she hadn't even thought about what to cook.

*Spaghetti it is.*

Not being in her own kitchen made something as simple as cooking spaghetti a chore. What should have only taken twenty minutes to make, took over an hour. The tiny kitchen held everything she needed, she just had to find it all.

The three glasses of wine didn't help. She had almost emptied the bottle Debbie had sent her. She'd never needed liquid courage before. This wasn't really courage to give in, but courage to say no.

Lisa was just putting the spaghetti into a large bowl then the knock came at her door. The sound made her heart speed up. She had so many things warring inside her.

She knew better than to spend any time with a fellow actor. Things never went well. But now, this guy could make or break her. And they were stuck together, divided only by a single wall, for the next... who knew how long. And he was hot. So fucking hot.

*How am I going to survive this?*

She took a deep breath and opened the door.

# CHAPTER 4

Kyle stood at the door to her apartment, unable to knock. He just stared at it, like it would open on its own. The chilled bottle of wine began to numb the fingers of his right hand.

*Just knock.*

He shifted the bottle from his hand to the crook of his arm. The other held a platter with two small bowls of chocolate pudding and a can of Reddi-Whip. Not to mention the six chocolate-covered strawberries.

Kyle looked down at the platter.

*Damn, maybe I tried too hard?*

Before he could change his mind, his hand reached up and rapped three times. He tried not to audibly gasp when she opened the door and he took her all in.

Dressed in a pair of fitted blue jeans, they could have been painted on. But her top was what flushed his body with heat. It was clear she had on no bra. Her nipples were taut, making an appearance through her shirts. Yes, shirts. She wore a white over-sized t-shirt that fell off her right shoulder, and a light pink tank top under that. Her black hair shone in light, the strands brought over her shoulders in a clear attempt to hide the fact she wore no bra. But it only helped to draw the eyes right there.

"Come on in," she said, stepping out of the way to allow him through.

He headed straight to the small kitchen to set down his tray. "Do you have room in the fridge for dessert? I'd hate for it to melt before we got to it."

She stepped around him to open the fridge door, the scent of her coconut shampoo filled his senses. He had to close his eyes and take a breath, trying to calm his body, but it just infused her deeper into him.

"Here, let me have it," she reached for the desserts.

Their fingers grazed when he handed it to her, sending a jolt of electricity through him.

Watching her set the tray in her fairly empty fridge, was almost his undoing.

She leaned down ever so slightly to slide the tray on the third shelf, her tight jeans showing every curve of her fine ass.

His eyes popped up to hers in a flash when she turned around, sure she had seen where his glance had been.

"Dinner smells great. Spaghetti?" he asked.

"I hope that's all right?"

"Of course. Would you like a glass of wine?"

She pointed to the glasses on the counter, the wine opener set before them.

He worked quickly to get the red liquid poured, knowing he needed a glass to try and cool himself down. It was going to be a long night.

Kyle held out her glass, noticing there was no place settings out yet.

Lisa was fluttering around the tiny kitchen, opening cupboards and drawers, then slamming them shut.

*So, she's flustered, too.*

"Can I help?"

She turned and let out a huff. "I can't find anything in this damned kitchen!"

He tried not to laugh. "Have a seat, Lisa. Take your wine," he handed it to her, watching her take a long, full drink of the red liquid. "Your kitchen is set up like mine. Let me take over."

It didn't take him long to find the plates and silverware, but her glass was empty when he stepped up to the table. He set everything out, returned to the counter to grab the bottle of wine, refilling her glass. It might be her place, but he took over the night. He dished out the pasta, not hesitating at the portions. She didn't seem like the type to nibble at her dinner to make an impression. Kyle slipped open the curtains she had closed. The view of the bay was beautiful, no matter the time of day. The sun had set and the lights on the water were breathtaking.

Kyle sat at the seat across from her and waited for her to make the first move.

It was another sip of wine.

He needed to break the tension that could be cut with a knife. Picking up his fork, Kyle filled it with pasta and shoved it in his mouth. He should have taken a small bite first. The noodles were not cooked. Al dente would be too nice to call it. These were still hard. He couldn't believe he hadn't noticed when he'd tried to twist them onto the fork. Chewing the best he could, it took half his glass of wine to get it all down.

Kyle refilled his glass, half the bottle now gone, and waited for her to acknowledge her disaster of a dinner. He would not bring it up. But to get away with not having to consume more, he began talking.

"Outstanding job on set today. I know these types of scenes are difficult. On anyone."

Lisa took a bite while Kyle continued.

"You handled it better than any woman I've had beneath me before."

Lisa began choking on her mouthful of pasta.

*Oh, shit!*

"Are you okay? Lisa?" He jumped up from his chair and ran to her side, pulling her out of her seat and over to the sink.

She leaned over the edge, still choking, but some food was falling into the stainless steel basin.

Kyle gently pat her on the back, not sure what to do.

*Oh my God, I've killed my leading lady!*

A few more violent coughs and she was reaching up to turn on the water in the sink, the last of her choking hazard evicted.

"I'm so sorry," they said at the same time when she finally stood back up and faced him.

"I didn't mean to…"

"I don't think I…"

They spoke at the same time again.

Lisa held up a hand to silence him when Kyle opened his mouth to speak.

"Let me go first." She took a deep breath, letting it out slowly. "It seems I undercooked the pasta. I can't say I have ever done that before. I am sorry for that. Seems I've ruined dinner."

"Then let's call it fair. I thought my comment had killed you. I brought dessert. It might not fill us up, but at least it's edible, right?"

Her cheeks flushed red. "I guess so." She moved to the table and began cleaning up, dumping the crispy noodles into the large pot it had started in. "I could make something else. I have some chicken, mushroom soup, and rice? It's kinda bland, but it's my little odd comfort food."

Kyle grabbed the dirty plates, taking them to the sink and began washing them. "It's all right. I'm really not hungry. Besides, we had a hell of a day and you really need not put yourself out. We can survive on chocolate pudding and whipped cream. I'll get it ready."

"Thank you. If you'll excuse me, I'll be right back."

He watched her rush to the bathroom. She hadn't looked like

she was going to be ill, but after what she had gone through, he wouldn't be surprised.

* * *

LISA STEPPED INTO THE BATHROOM, turned on the light and shut the door. The moment she saw her face, she gasped.

*No wonder he's being so nice! I look like death!*

Black streaks framed her white face from her makeup running, but her cheeks were flushed red. She grabbed a washcloth and worked quickly to clean her face up.

*Well, he's seen me at my worst now. No point in trying to look good anymore.*

Lisa scrubbed her skin clean, applied a little lotion and chapstick, then headed back out to him. She had already ruined the night. What more could go wrong?

She stepped out to see Kyle sitting on the couch, one ankle resting on the other knee, and the tray of desserts sitting in front of him. On either side of that was their glasses of wine, now completely full. The only place to sit in the tiny apartment was the couch, so she let out the breath she hadn't realized she was holding in, and joined him. There wasn't much room between the two of them. There was no way three people could fit on it comfortably. She was sure if either of them shifted slightly, their knees would touch. She made the mistake of taking a deep breath. His musky scent was intoxicating

He smiled, leaning over to grab her wine and offer it to her.

*Is he trying to get me drunk? I think I already am, just from being near him*

"Are you all right, now? That was rather scary. I've never had someone choke in front of me."

She was positive her cheeks were bright red. She took a sip before replying. "I've never undercooked my pasta then tried to kill myself with it. But yes, I'm all right. Are you sure you don't want me to cook something else?" She wasn't hungry, but getting back into the kitchen would get her away from him, and the hot mess he was making her, even if it was only a few feet away. She took another big sip of her wine.

"Yes. I'm sure. Here, try this," he said, reaching for the pudding. "It's my grandma's recipe. You don't really need the whipped cream, but it makes for a good presentation. Should I add some?"

The way he spoke to her made her body sing. He wasn't trying to seduce her. He could have suggested an extremely erotic way to enjoy the pudding and whipped cream, but he didn't. He was simply being a person, offering her a family treat.

*So why is it making me wet?*

She set down the wine glass and took the small dish and spoon before he could add the whipped cream, then scooped a very small bite. She'd learned her lesson watching Kyle with the pasta. But the moment the chocolate touched her tongue, an explosion of pleasure assaulted her senses. She couldn't help a moan that slipped from her lips.

"I told ya it was good."

She gave him a weak smile before taking another spoonful. "Oh my God, it is completely sinful. Your grandmother used to make this?"

"She still does. It's only for special occasions, but anytime I get to see her, which is usually only at Christmas, she makes a big batch."

"What's the special occasion now, then?" she couldn't help but ask before taking another spoonful into her mouth.

He was silent a moment, so she looked over at him. It surprised her to see his cheeks were flushed, and he was looking down into his pudding.

*Where is Mr. Playboy?*

"I… um… I thought it might be a nice way to welcome you to the set."

"Do you do this for all your love interests?" Her voice was a little more harsh than she had meant.

He was being so nice. But was it part of his seduction?

She wouldn't be another actress he put into his collection of hook-ups.

Kyle's head snapped up; he'd heard the underline hints in her voice, she was sure of it.

"No. I don't." The tone in his voice confirmed her suspicions. He'd heard her, in more ways than one. "You know what, maybe I should go. It's been a long day. I'll check on you tomorrow." He stood up and walked out, leaving behind his dessert tray and half a glass of wine.

# CHAPTER 5

Lisa polished off her glass of wine, then poured another and downed that one. She's screwed things up worse than before. She kept reminding herself she needed to make him like her.

Without letting him seduce her.

He could make or break her in Vancouver.

And she was making it easy for him to hate her.

She finished her pudding, then began devouring his. If he was going to leave it behind, she couldn't let it go to waste. She was halfway through his bowl when there was a knock on the door.

*What the fuck does he want? His dessert? Too bad, I ate it.*

She flung open the door, fueled by the wine she'd consumed, practically a full bottle, with nothing to eat but pudding. "What do you…"

She didn't get to finish her sentence.

Kyle stepped up to her, slipped one hand on her waist, around to her lower back, and the other delved into her black hair, gripping tight. He pulled her to him, slamming their bodies together as he stole her breath with a fiery kiss.

She couldn't break away.

She didn't want to.

He was all around her, from his heady scent, to his rock hard body.

She was ready to drag him back inside and seduce him.

Kyle broke the kiss and let her go, stepping back out of her reach. "I'm sick and tired of being accused of being a player on set. I have never pursued a woman I've worked with before. Not until you. I don't know what you do to me. I don't know how to handle this. So I thought I would just be upfront and tell you. So, yeah. Um... goodnight."

His apartment door slammed closed with him behind it before she had even caught her breath.

Lisa lay in bed for hours, staring at the ceiling, wondering what the hell to do with the information she had been given. Did she believe him when he said he wasn't the player, but the one being played?

Yes, she did.

After spending part of a night with him, really seeing him, he wasn't trying to seduce her. He'd just been kind. And she was the one fighting to control herself around him. She didn't want to be a notch on his bedpost, yet she was drawn to him. She could see how other women on set would want him. Maybe she did have it all turned around.

*What am I going to do?*

STUMBLING TO HER KITCHEN, Lisa grumbled to herself that morning came too early, even though her watch said ten am. She got a pot of coffee brewing and headed for the bathroom. She might still be half asleep, but she couldn't miss the white envelope on her dark hardwood floors, still partially under the front door. She leaned down to pick it up, becoming dizzy when she stood back up too quickly.

*No wine today, please. No wine.*

She stepped into the bathroom and opened the note.

The handwriting was perfect print, so well done it could have been written by a man or a woman. She knew it was from Kyle, even before beginning to read.

LISA,

   *Please forgive me for my behavior last night.*
   *It was uncalled for.*
   *I don't know why I'm so affected by you.*
   *If you will let me make it up to you, we could have lunch today.*
   *My place.*
   *1pm.*


*Kyle*


SHE STARED AT THE NOTE, rereading it three times.

   *I need coffee.*

Carrying the paper back to the kitchen, Lisa got a cup of joe and headed to her balcony. It was a nice morning, warm for March, and curled up in the padded chair in the corner.

She wasn't there long before she heard the sliding glass door from the balcony beside hers opening. She glanced over to see Kyle stepping out onto his deck. He hadn't seen her yet, and she wasn't about to draw attention to her location. She was enjoying the view.

He had no shirt on. And his grey sweatpants sat low, showing the delicious line on his hips she would love to lick.

   *Stop that!*

Lisa could completely understand why the women on set had wanted to bed him. It had been the last thing on her mind when she arrived, and the first thing she thought of since meeting him.

*And I'm gonna have lunch with him?*

She reached up and touched her lips, remembering the surprise from the night before. She hadn't seen it coming, and was unable to react before he took off. She still wasn't sure what it had all been about. That was part of what drew her to accept his proposal for lunch. She also knew it could lead to other things.

Was she willing to let that happen?

Was she willing to pass up the chance?

Lisa waited for him to return inside before escaping indoors herself, where she dressed with care, preparing to 'go have lunch'.

"THIS PLACE IS SO MUCH NICER than my apartment," she whispered more to herself than anything when she stepped into his unit a few hours later. She looked around at the living room, complete with a huge flat screen tv across from a deep chocolate leather sofa.

"I'm glad you came. I really didn't think you would. Here, let me show you around," Kyle said gleefully.

He'd been right the other day when he said the layout was the same, but mirrored. But he had much nicer things in his place. Including the bathroom.

"So, the shower was custom done to fit my height. Have you ever noticed most shower heads are less than six feet from the floor," he said when she looked inside. He leaned his six-foot three-inch frame over her shoulder and continued. "I always said I thought it was big enough for two people and they didn't need to build it that way. Maybe we'll have to try later and see." He said it so low she wasn't entirely sure she'd heard him right.

Lisa felt her cheeks flush and goosebumps erupt all the way into her hairline. It was intoxicating being that close to him.

He shut the door and led her into his bedroom. The bed was

small, maybe a queen, with a comforter that matched the color of the living room sofa.

She turned slightly to ask him how he fit on the small bed, but didn't realize how close he was and she smacked into his hard chest. She felt her cheeks flush at the contact. She looked up at him, watching the dimple in his cheek play peekaboo. She was afraid to look into his eyes.

"You okay?" he asked, a knowing smile spreading.

She could only nod.

He slipped his hand over her cheek, his thumb ever so slightly caressing her soft skin as he brought her gently in for a kiss. His lips embraced her own while the hint of scruff tickled her chin. He wrapped a hand around her waist and pulled her body against his.

Lisa felt her body stir and butterflies flutter. Her breasts felt extra sensitive pressed against him. This wasn't why she came over, to be seduced.

She wanted to stop him.

No, she didn't.

She wanted him to go on.

She didn't think she would ever get over the thrill of his kisses or the heady scent of musk. Her body was so alive, just being near him. They were fully clothed, and she could still feel the building within her body. If they went much further than just simple kissing, she would surely explode.

Lisa could hardly breathe when Kyle slid down the zipper of her blue dress. He kissed each bare shoulder as he went. She helped to remove the dress and half-slip leaving her with only white satin bloomers.

He laughed quietly before commenting. "Not at all what I thought you'd be wearing under your dress. They look like something a grandma would wear."

Lisa turned around to face him, slipping her arms around his neck. She stood on her tippy toes and kissed him softly, whispering against his lips. "You know you find them sexy. Besides, they keep my thighs from chafing."

He didn't reply, Kyle just kissed her with such an intense passion that it took her breath away. There was no denying it; he wanted her as much as she was fighting with herself about how much she wanted him.

Her hands slipped away to find the hem of his shirt. She let the material gather on her wrists as her fingers trailed up his six-pack to his pecks, feeling his nipples pucker.

Kyle shuddered at her light touch, further fueling her desire.

She wanted to torture him; she moved slowly and kept her touch light. Lisa pulled off his shirt and dropped it on the floor, smiling as he ran his fingers through his hair to smooth it back down. Just then, she reached for his belt and unbuckled it. She looked up into his deep green eyes, biting her lower lip as she opened his pants.

Lisa slipped her hand in, freeing him, and began gently stroking his thick shaft.

Kyle's head tipped back and he moaned in pleasure.

Lisa kept up her sweet assault, but only for a moment when Kyle put his hands on her waist. "Please," he said in a raspy voice. "I can't take it."

She released him but hooked her fingers into the waistband of his jeans and boxer briefs and slowly began peeling them down his legs, lowering her body as she went. She helped him step out of them and looked up at him.

He offered her his hand and helped her to her feet. As he stood before her, completely naked, all she wanted to do was wrap her arms around him and hold him tight, skin to skin. Her hands went to the center to his chest, where she splayed them out before sweeping them around to his back. Pressing her bare breasts against his chest, she shivered when his fingers lightly trailed up and down her back.

Their eyes held each other a moment longer until Kyle

shocked her by sweeping her off her feet and carrying her to the bed. He laid her down so gently, then grabbed her bloomers and pulled them off in one swift movement.

Lisa laughed as he threw them over his shoulder and joined her on the bed.

Kyle gently nudged her knees apart so he could rest there as he leaned on his elbows on either side of her.

She reached up and pushed a lock of hair back behind his ear before pulling him down for a deep kiss. When Lisa released him, she wrapped her long legs around his torso, not only to give him access, but simply because it was more comfortable on her hips.

Her hands slid up and down his back, a gentle caress that sent shivers over his skin. Lisa felt him shift, ever so slightly, to press against her core, testing her readiness. She had been wet since they entered his bedroom.

Kyle pressed forward very slightly, then pulled back a moment later before entering her again. His eyes went wide, completely taken by surprise when she thrust her hips upward and pulled his body down, trying to get her fill of him.

Lisa was so aroused she didn't need or want Kyle to take his time. She needed him, fully in her, without hesitation. Her fingers pressed hard into his back as she urged him on. She wasn't one for pillow talk, but she found herself calling out to him.

"Kyle!" She cried out. "More! Oh!" She kept thrusting upwards with each of his strokes down, trying to take him deeper. She wasn't thinking when she begged him to thrust harder, faster, taking him deeper into her body. She felt her body tensing up, her orgasm so close, so soon. Lisa went rigid as her body tightened around him, preparing to explode.

He stopped thrusting when he realized she was no longer moving with him.

"Lisa, are you okay," he asked worriedly.

She laughed. "Yes. Damn! I was so close!"

He looked at her with curiosity written in the crease of his brow, not quite understanding.

She didn't explain, she just pushed at his chest to get him to roll over and onto his back. She straddled him then, not giving him a moment to think before she impaled herself upon him and began riding him hard and fast.

Kyle was so thick. He filled her tight sheath, sending delicious sensations throughout her body. He reached up to caress her breasts, gently running his thumbs back and forth across her highly sensitive nipples, causing her to tighten around him.

Lisa rocked on his hips, taking him so deep.

He bucked slightly under her, pushing deeper. She came down hard onto him as he pushed up and only a few more thrusts together and her core tightened around him.

She continued to move with her orgasm. Riding it out as long as she could. Lisa felt Kyle's body twitched under her as his own orgasm exploded.

Lisa eventually collapsed forward onto his chest, burying her face into his neck, breathing in their combined scent. She was panting, her breath ragged. Her hand slid up his chest and she could feel his heart thunder against her palm. "So," she whispered, her face still buried. "Shall we try out that shower?"

# CHAPTER 6

Kyle hadn't intended to take advantage of the bedroom in his apartment. He truly had honorable intentions. He wanted to show her their places were mirrored. But when they walked into his personal oasis, a place he had never shared with a lady friend, something came over him. It wasn't just his body that craved her, although the urges were strong enough. He wanted to be close to her, as close as one could be.

Lisa followed him into his bathroom and sat on the edge of the small tub while she started the water.

He got down on one knee to get them both towels from under the sink, setting them on the tub beside her. When he stood back up at his full height, she reached for him, grabbing his bicep and brought him down to capture his soft lips. His hands splayed across her back as their tongues danced with each other.

She released his face to reach in between them, leaning forward to breathe hot air on his throbbing member. It bounced up and down of its own accord, making her giggle.

Kyle was caught off guard when Lisa took him into her mouth.

She slid her hands up the outside of his legs and he sucked in his breath.

He let out a hiss of pleasure when she took his sac into her hand and gently massaged it. He couldn't believe how skilled she was with her mouth. He wanted to let her continue but the water was running.

"Lisa, I can't... The water..."

She released him, but hadn't risen when he reached to check on the water. When he turned back to face her, she just smiled at him.

He offered her a hand and she stepped into the delicious water, Kyle followed right behind her.

Kyle wanted to make love to her again and started to get her all hot and bothered by simply washing her. He caressed and rinsed, making sure no part of her was left untouched. He watched her wriggle and writhe. Perhaps she wanted it as much as he did. And though the shower was large, he wanted to be so deep in her, he'd never achieve that standing there.

He stepped out of the shower first and rather than dry himself off, he motioned for Lisa to step out. He wrapped the large fluffy purple towel around her and began rubbing her dry. He took his time, as he stood there dripping, making sure every spot on her was seen to.

Every spot but one.

He had dried the top of her feet, then her calves, then her thighs. When he reached the junction between her legs, he dropped the towel.

Lisa's hands slid along Kyle's short wet hair as his fingers found her wet spot. She moaned in pleasure as he teased her body slowly. He was doing his job well, causing her hands to grip his shoulders for balance. She dug her nails into his flesh.

*Pain is just pleasure with the volume up.*

*I want it louder.*

He gently prodded her legs further apart so he could place his tongue where his fingers had been. But only a moment later, Lisa's legs grew weak. He could see her knees shaking. He stood up and walked her to the bedroom, laying her back on the bed with her feet still on the floor. Kyle knelt on the carpet, putting him right at the perfect level to finish what he'd started.

Kyle began tasting her again.

Lisa placed her feet on his chest, giving him full access to her body.

He dug in, enjoying every inch of her womanhood.

He breathed her in, never wanting to forget her scent, it would help him get him through the long days without her. He felt her body tense up as her orgasm built. His fingers joined his mouth as he helped her over the edge.

She cried out his name and threw back her head, her body pulsating around his digits.

He didn't stop then, he kept going, helping her ride out the delicious wave. He left her panting for breath as she tried to sit up.


LISA SMILED AT KYLE SEDUCTIVELY, curling her finger at him to get him to join her on the mattress. She might have orgasmed, but she was just getting started.

He came to stand beside the bed, looking down at her, his eyes blazing with heat, green fire. He sat on the edge and leaned over to kiss her softly.

Her hands found their way to his neck where she held him as they shared the tender moment. She reached down to gently grasp his throbbing manhood. She teased him, softly running her hand up and down the hard shaft. It felt like velvet over steel.

He sucked in a breath when their lips parted.

She whispered to him, "Turnabout is fair play."

He kissed her hard then, like he was enticing her to tease his body a bit more. But then she was surprised when he put his hand over hers, ceasing her actions.

"I appreciate that, and it's not that I don't want reciprocation, but it's not about me right now. Let me take care of you." His voice was so sincere, the light in his eyes so bright, she felt her heart soar.

This was such a novelty in her world.

She couldn't speak, only nod as he adjusted himself on the bed, placing himself between her legs.

Kyle rested on his elbows, his hands finding their way into her baby-soft hair. He looked at her with such longing, she felt her cheeks flush.

*How did I get here?*

She still couldn't believe it.

He pressed so gently at her core like he wasn't sure if she needed to be brought back to life, but there was no need.

She was quite ready for him.

He slipped in with ease.

Lisa wrapped her legs around his waist as he began a slow, yet deep rhythm. Once again he was taking his time with her, making sure she was satisfied. Her hands slid to his fine backside, where she felt his muscles flex with each deep push into her. Her face buried in his hair when he came down closer to her. They both breathed in, the combined scent filling them. It was heady and only fueled their passion more.

Kyle stopped moving. "I want to try something new," he whispered. He adjusted them so that Lisa was on top, with her knees on either side of his hips. But rather than laying on his back, he was also in a sitting position.

Her hands explored his back while he tenderly held her cheeks to be able to assault her with sweet tender kisses. It was the most intimate thing she had ever done. It felt so personal to be with him in that moment, sharing more than just their bodies, she felt like their souls were connecting.

Lisa had control over the motion, being the one to move the way her body liked it most. Her head went back as her body began building and he leaned forward to taste the hollow of her neck, the curve of her shoulder, her earlobe. Her nails dug into his back as her body once again exploded, her sheath quivered around him. In one swift movement, he had her flat on her back as he drove deep and hard, finding his own release as her aftershocks rocked her. He collapsed onto her, not fully, most of his weight still on his arms.

"Thank you," was all he said.

Lisa wasn't sure what he was thanking her for. She felt she should be thanking him. But one thing she was sure about. He wasn't a playboy. But he could play her.

# EPILOGUE

Six weeks.

That's how long the city stayed under strict lockdown.

Airports hadn't opened yet, most shops and restaurants were still closed. And filming had not resumed. Lisa hadn't left her apartment building since the first day when she'd gone to the store. She hadn't needed to. Between what she had in her place, and what Kyle had in his, they wanted for nothing.

Except for chocolate pudding.

They sat at the kitchen table, ham and cheese sandwiches, potato chips, and now warm soda, covered the tabletop. Neither one of them had a stitch on, and they were all right with that. They spent most of their days naked.

"So, what happens now," Lisa asked, the news playing quietly in the background.

"I think it's still not safe to go out."

"You want to stay here longer? Don't you want to leave?"

He smiled at her, that damned dimple playing havoc with her hormones. "No."

"Why not?" she pushed.

"Because then we'd have to put clothes on. And I've really loved acting the part."

She looked at him a moment, trying to understand his words. "Acting the part?"

He stood up, walking over to stand right beside her, his growing erection right at her level of contact. "Like we are the only two people left in the world or the first two people. And I'm hungry."

She looked at his untouched sandwich.

His gaze followed hers.

"It's not a sandwich I'm craving."

She could play along. She pushed at him to take a step back to allow her to stand. Rather than reaching for him, she stepped into the kitchen and picked up something from the counter. When she turned around, she offered it to him, pressing her bare breasts together for enticement.

"Wanna bite of my apple?"

"Why, yes, Eve. I think I do."

# ABOUT THE AUTHOR

Andrea Hurtt is an emerging author of various romance categories. She enjoys writing a little bit of everything.

She's still deciding what she wants to be when she grows up. Andrea has been a dental assistant, a stay at home mom, owned her own clothing store, was a clothing designer with a vintage inspired clothing line, Amaryllis Designs, even won Omaha Fashion Week for Top Designer in her category, and Top Boutique for Cancer Survivor Night.

Shea spends her days either writing books and screenplays, or making #EmotionalSupportPillows and traveling withy he cast and fans of the CWTV show Supernatural.

Andrea recently moved to Vancouver, Canada for a year to start her acting and screenplay career, and has won 10 awards for her screenwriting scripts.

She is the mother of two children, has a cat and a dog, and is a proud Army wife, currently residing in the Midwest.

For more books and updates:
Facebook.com/andreahurttauthor
Twitter.com/atomicbombshel1
Instagram.com/andreahurttactor
Amazon.com/author/andreahurtt

 twitter.com/atomicbombshel1

# ALSO BY ANDREA HURTT

*Razor's Edge Rockstar Romance*

*Masquerade - Book 1*

*Undone - Book 1.5*

*Unmistakable - Book 2*

*Incomplete - Book 3*

**Coming Soon**

*Razor's Edge Rockstar Romance*

*Drowning - Book 4*

*Inconsolable - Book 5*

*The Sealgaire Saga*

*A Slice of Hell - Book 1*

*Prince Cove Curse*

*Under The Sea - Book 1*